mango's Quest

the story of a home lost and found

By Ralph da Costa Nunez
with Robyn Schwartz

Introduction by Leonard N. Stern

Illustrated by Amarides Montgomery

White Tiger Press
New York

Introduction

Mango's Quest is the fifth in a series of children's books specifically aimed at teaching children about the experience of being homeless. Why is this important? Because most people don't know that the typical homeless person in America today is a child. Sadly, over one million children will be homeless tonight, and their numbers continue to grow.

As you read about Mango the hamster, you and your children will learn what homelessness is, and see the fear and sadness that comes with not having a home. The support the school community provides for Mango will teach children how they can help those less fortunate than themselves.

I cannot think of a better educational tool than a children's book about homeless animals to introduce young people to this poverty that has become so prevalent in our society. It is my hope that someday such a book will no longer be needed. Working together, we can make that happen.

Leonard N. Stern
Founder/Chairman
Homes for the Homeless, New York City

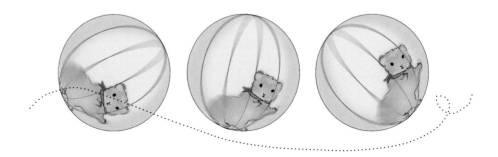

Hi there readers! Keep an eye out for Mango's orange paw prints throughout this story. While there are many words that you will recognize in this book, there may be a few that are unfamiliar. Each paw print lies next to a key vocabulary word. At the end of the story, you will find Mango's word list that includes simplified definitions with suggested topics and questions for discussion.

A special note about family homelessness: while the issue of homelessness can be a difficult topic for children, this book can help you begin the conversation in a child-friendly way. Please visit the Institute for Children and Poverty online at **www.icpny.org** for further reading on this subject.

Happy reading!

Everyone knows hamsters like to run, but Mango was special.

Mango loved to run.

Mango was soft, furry, friendly, and tall. He was the pride and joy of the second graders in Room 222.

1

Mango lived in Room 222 with his friends Peaches and Tangerine, and their family of hamster pups.

He loved to spend his <u>waking hours</u> running, but he always made time to play with the growing pups.

2

Mango, Peaches, Tangerine, and the pups all lived in a wire cage filled with soft wood chips and a speedy silver wheel where Mango loved to run. *But as the pups got bigger and bigger, they all had less and less room. Their hamster cage was getting <u>crowded</u>.*

3

The day finally came when Tangerine and Peaches had to face the <u>facts</u>. Tangerine sadly explained to Mango, *"We just don't have enough room anymore. I'm afraid you're going to have to find yourself a new <u>home</u>."*

"But where will I go?"

Mango asked, feeling confused, sad, and shaky inside. Tangerine hugged him and said, "I don't know. I just don't know."

4

That night, after the second graders in Room 222 were long gone and his hamster friends had gone to sleep, Mango took a big sip of water, stuffed his cheeks full with food, and nosed his way out of the top of the cage.

"Where can a little hamster like me find a new place to live?"

Mango asked himself as he set off on a quest to find a home of his own.

5

Down the hall, Mango spied Finny the Fish in his beautiful glass aquarium.

"Finny, I have no place to run and no place to sleep. May I stay with you tonight?" Mango asked.

"I'd like to help you, Mango, but we already have too many fish in our bowl. Besides, you would have a hard time running or sleeping underwater."

Farther down the hallway, Mango found Lucy the Lizard in her cozy terrarium. "Lucy, I have no place to run or sleep. May I stay with you tonight?"

"Gee, Mango, I wish you could, but there are already four other lizards in this small tank. We sleep with sun lamps on all the time, and it's way too hot for running," Lucy answered.

Lucy's
Rock

Next, he came across Pepper the Parakeet in his bright golden cage.

"Pepper, I need a place to run and a place to sleep. May I stay with you tonight?" Mango asked.

"I'm sorry, but this cage is made for just one bird. Besides, there's no wheel for you to run on, and you wouldn't be able to sleep on my swing."

8

"But where will I go, there is no place for me anywhere!" Mango cried.

Pepper squawked back, "It seems to me that you're homeless." "Homeless? What is that?" Mango asked.

"It means you have no place to live, no home of your own," Pepper replied.

"Well, I guess I'm homeless then," Mango said with tears in his eyes.

9

"Wait!" Pepper shouted. "Have you heard of the Mouse House?" Mango suddenly felt better. "What is that? Where is it?"

"It's a place you can go when you don't have a home. You'll see a tiny entrance in the corner of the library. In there you will find a warm bed for tonight and maybe even a place to run."

"Thanks, Pepper. I'm off to the Mouse House," Mango called out as he headed toward the library.

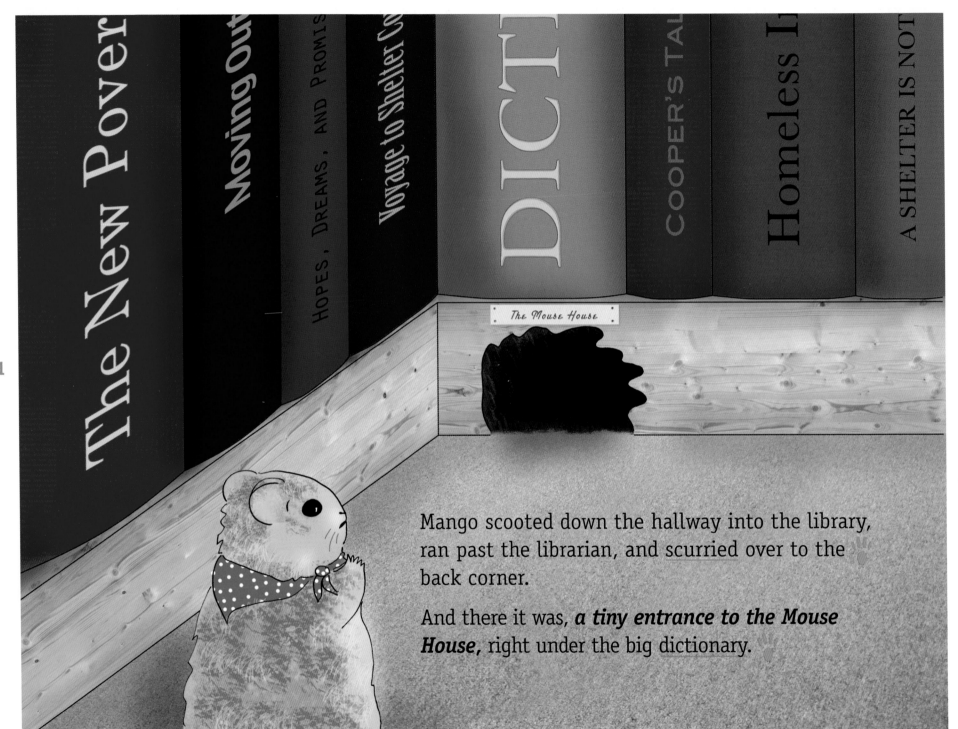

The books on the shelf read:

The New Pover[ty]
Moving Out
HOPES, DREAMS, AND PROMIS[ES]
Voyage to Shelter Co[ve]
DICTI[ONARY]
COOPER'S TAL[E]
Homeless
A SHELTER IS NOT

The Mouse House

Mango scooted down the hallway into the library, ran past the librarian, and scurried over to the back corner.

And there it was, **a tiny entrance to the Mouse House**, right under the big dictionary.

Slowly, Mango crawled toward the
small hole in the wall and whispered firmly,

"Hello there. I need a place to stay."

Before Mango could blink, a kindly old pack rat named Paulie Packrat came out the hole carrying a long list of names.

"What's your name and where did you come from?" he asked.

"I'm Mango. I think I'm homeless. I used to live with Tangerine, Peaches, and the hamster pups, but our cage got <u>overcrowded</u> and I had to leave."

"Well, Mango, you came to the right place. *The Mouse House is full of creatures without homes*."

Inside there were homeless ants in community ant farms, homeless spiders spinning community webs, and homeless guinea pigs with community hutches. In the corner there was a community pile of wood chips for homeless hamsters, where Mango quickly fell asleep.

14

The next morning when the second graders arrived to Room 222 they discovered that Mango was missing. They were all very worried.

"What do you think happened to him, Ms. Cookie?" Jesse asked his teacher.

"I'm not sure. Maybe the hamster cage just got too crowded for him," she said.

"*I know what that feels like. I used to live in an overcrowded home,*" said Lisa. "When my mom got sick we had to move in with my aunt. But seven people living in a small apartment became a problem. It was hard living doubled-up, and we had to leave."

"Where did you go?" asked Mary Louise.

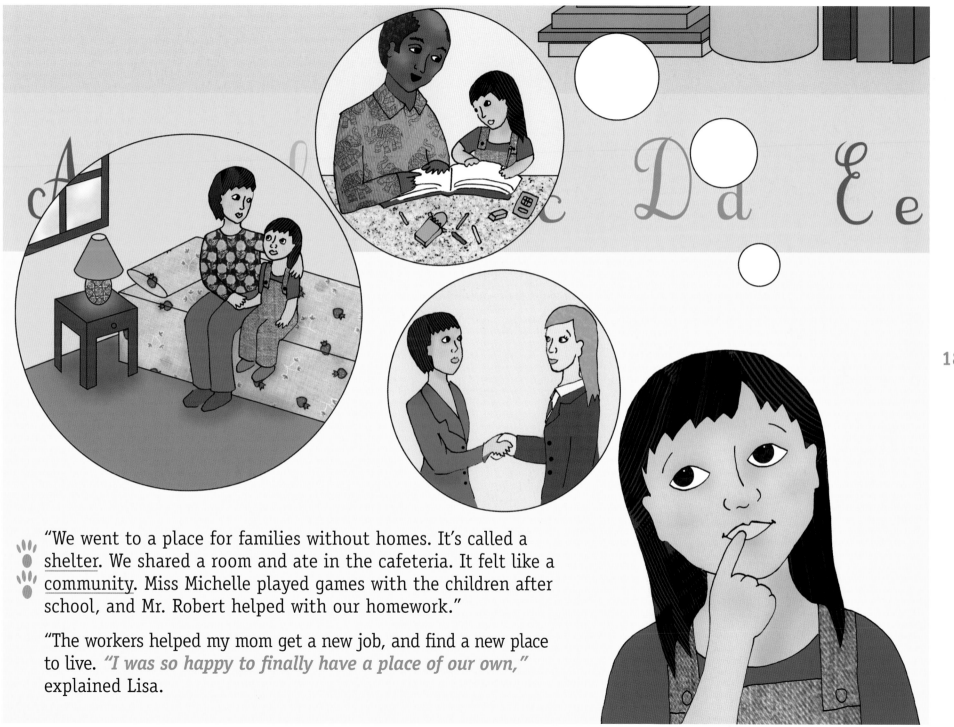

"We went to a place for families without homes. It's called a shelter. We shared a room and ate in the cafeteria. It felt like a community. Miss Michelle played games with the children after school, and Mr. Robert helped with our homework."

"The workers helped my mom get a new job, and find a new place to live. *"I was so happy to finally have a place of our own,"* explained Lisa.

"I hope Mango finds a shelter," said Anna. "But we should still try to find him and bring him back."

"Does anyone have any ideas for how we can help Mango find a new place to live?" asked Miss Cookie.

19

The children were eager to help. "We have an old hamster cage at my house!" shouted Jerry. "I'll get a water bottle for it," offered Mario. "I can get some wood chips for Mango to sleep on," said Maya.

"That's great," said Miss Cookie, "now we just need to find Mango."

Back at the Mouse House, **Mango was learning all about shelters.** Paulie Packrat's office was filled with lists of animals' names and places where they could find new homes.

"Mango, maybe you can help me with my pile of lists today? I need help finding new homes for lizards."

"I would love to," said Mango.

Meanwhile the students of Room 222 began searching for Mango.
"Have you seen our hamster?" *they asked everyone they saw.*
"He is soft, furry, friendly, and tall.
His name is Mango and he loves to run."

It was Mr. Peachtree who finally spotted Mango running outside the Mouse House.

"Hey there, Mango, a whole lot of kids have been looking for you! Room 222 wants you to come home."

Mr. Peachtree put Mango in his front shirt pocket. "So long, Paulie Packrat!" Mango called out.

"Thank you for all of your help!"

Paulie Packrat waved, and checked Mango off his list. He had helped another homeless animal in his search to find a place to live.

PEACHTREE

Mango and Mr. Peachtree headed to Room 222. The class was thrilled to have Mango back.

Mr. Peachtree smiled and said, *"Everyone, including a furry, friendly hamster, needs a home."*

The next morning, Ms. Cookie helped the children build Mango's new home. Jerry's old hamster cage was perfect, and it even had a big wheel. Maya's water bottle fit just right. Mario's wood chips covered the entire cage floor. The children put Mango's new cage next to the one shared by Tangerine and Peaches's family. *Mango's eyes lit up at the sight of his new home and his old friends.*

"Welcome back, Mango!" Tangerine said. "It's great to have you as a neighbor, and I'm sorry you became homeless." Mango smiled, "It's good to be back! No one should be homeless—no one. But I understand why I had to leave. I even made some new friends while I was gone."

After running all day long on his big new wheel, Mango burrowed into the soft wood chips and began to <u>drift</u> off to sleep.

Later, the class discussed what they had learned from Mango's and Lisa's experiences and decided to help other students learn about homelessness.

Just then, Mango whispered, "We are all part of a community, and it takes a community to end homelessness."

mango's word list

Community: *n.* A social group of any size whose members share a common place to live, a common culture, or common beliefs.
Mango whispered: "It takes a <u>community</u> to end homelessness."

Crowded: *adj.* Uncomfortably close together.
Tangerine sighed, "Mango, it's too <u>crowded</u> in here, and we just don't have enough room."

Dictionary: *n.* A book where you can find what words mean, how to spell them, and how to use them.
"There was the Mouse House, right under the big <u>dictionary</u>."

Doubled-up: *adj.* When two families or more are sharing a single living space.
Lisa said, "It was hard living <u>doubled-up</u>, and we had to leave."

Drift: *v.* To be carried along, as if by air or water.
'Drifting off to sleep' is a popular saying, meaning that one is carried off to sleep. *"Mango smiled as he <u>drifted</u> off to sleep."*

Fact: *n.* Something that is true.
The popular saying 'face the facts' means that you have to accept what is true, even if that is difficult to do. "One day, Peaches and Tangerine had to face the <u>facts</u>."

Home: *n.* The place where you live.
Everyone, even a hamster, needs a <u>home</u> of his or her own.

Homeless: *adj.* A person without a place to live.
Pepper the Parrot squawked: "It looks to me like you're <u>homeless</u>, Mango. You have no place to live, no home of your own."

Housing: *n.* A place to live.
Lisa's family moved into a temporary shelter and eventually found permanent <u>housing</u>.

Overcrowded: *adj.* Having too many people in one place. Similar to doubled-up.
"I know something about living in an <u>overcrowded</u> home," Lisa said.

Quest: *n.* An adventure in search of something or someone.
"Mango set off on a <u>quest</u> to find a home."

Scurry: *v.* To move quickly and low to the ground.
"Mango <u>scurried</u> across the library floor."

Shelter: *n.* A place where homeless families can get help and live for a short time.
"We went to a place for families without homes. It's called a <u>shelter</u>."

Terrarium: *n.* A glass container for plants and/or animals.
Further down the hallway, Mango found Lucy the Lizard in her cozy <u>terrarium</u>.

Waking hours: *n.* The time spent when one is not asleep.
"Mango loved to spend his <u>waking hours</u> running."

Questions for discussion:

1. Why did Mango leave Tangerine's cage? Discuss the concept of "overcrowding" and of living "doubled-up."

2. Does a shelter, like the Mouse House or the one Lisa describes, seem like a good place to stay?

3. What does Mango mean when he says that "it takes a community to end homelessness"? Do you think that Mango is right?

4. How could you end homelessness in your community?

Mango's Quest is the fifth in a series of children's book published by White Tiger Press. Each book addresses the issue of homelessness and poverty, and the approachable story lines make ideal points for discussion.

Read and collect all five!

Look for our series at your local library. All of our publications are available for purchase online at the Institute for Children and Poverty Web site, www.icpny.org.